Medicine and Other Stories
Femdom Mind Control
Flash Fiction – Vol. 16

S.B.

Table of Contents

The best treatment in the world awaits you

A special 'Thank you' to all patrons of Spell... B-O-U-ND.

2 o'clock Appointment

Oh, hello. Didn't notice you standing there. Are you the 2 o'clock appointment? I'm afraid you're going to have to wait for a while because the doctor is stuck in traffic. In the meantime, why don't you sit in that chair over there? Or do you prefer to stand and look at my computer screen just like you're doing right now? It's your call. Do as you please.

So... do you like my personalized screensaver? I made it myself, you know? It's great for when I'm feeling down or tired. It helps me clear up my mind, relax, and see rainbows when everyone else sees dark clouds of storm. Just a few seconds are enough to put things in perspective again. I was looking at it before you came in but I'm a person who loves to share so... look all you want...

Yes, stare at the glimmering colors... they're so lovely, aren't they? Apologies if I'm talking too much... it's just I'm so proud of my creation, especially the way the colorful swirls irradiate perfectly from the center of the image... It's no surprise you were drawn to it as soon as you came in the room, and who can blame you for choosing to stand instead of sitting, for trying to know the pattern from inside out and let it know you as well? So easy to keep staring, even easier to keep listening, letting this feeling own your spirit little by little, introducing subtle variations to your way of thinking...

I know that by now all you really desire is to be one with the screensaver, to have it swirl endlessly inside your feeble brain and to listen and accept the sound of my voice as a beautiful melody played in the key of hypnosis but, for that, I need you to come closer so you can feast on the flashing colors merging into one another from the most perfect angle available. Approach my chair, yes... knees buckling, head tilted to the left... wonderful! Now, allow your legs to succumb to the weight of your body. Kneel in front of the powerful spiraling picture and the even more irresistible woman who designed it.

Hmm... it's so delightful to have a man at my feet! I learned it with the good doctor who loves to implant her will on the weak ones under the guise of therapy... Had she been here on time, you would have become hers for sure. Am I lucky or what? An unexpected break, and a new slave... I love my job!

A Dream Come True

It was the strangest day in Trevor's life, and he had had a few. Working in retail for a decade exposes people to all the good, bad, and weird in the world, the latter of which produces stories no one will believe unless they live them. He loved to record them for posterity, a journal of the uncanny with an extra picture or two. Someday, he would compile them all, publish them online and boom, instant millionaire!

"Yeah, right... Keep telling yourself that..." he muttered as he exited the crowded New York subway, notebook in hand. A sketch of an old, angry woman with a hole in her face mask so she could "exercise her constitutional right to breathe" dominated the page he was looking at, sunken eyes in need of a good night's sleep. She was the latest 'acquisition' in his compendium of idiocy, though certainly not the last until the year was done.

Aged 31, Trevor's primary dreams were: move to a place where he could own three dogs, buy a vintage Pontiac Astre and open a bookstore of his own, not necessarily in that order. Sometimes, he also dreamed of being captured by a mysterious woman, a silent Goddess that wanted nothing else except his mindless compliance, but he never talked about those for there was no point.

Head down, still trying to figure out what else to add to his sketch, Trevor could have easily missed the moment when his dreams came true had he not been pushed to the side by the wave of working drones behind him, a proof that the best things in life are often born of accidents. He was stumbling like a fool when he saw her.

She stood by an escalator, dressed in a semi-transparent gray latex dress, curls of silky auburn hair resting on soft, incredibly feminine shoulders. Her face was hidden from view, though he was sure it was as stunning as the rest of the package. Although she appeared to be completely still, a closer look would reveal a sultry sway of hips. The innuendos of her latex-clad ass were mesmerizing. Bathed in soft light, it was as if they were a beacon in the night but hell-bent on making ships sink instead of guiding them to a safe shore.

Trevor had one chance to look away and, a single moment between a blink and the next stare, as tiny as a drop of water on an endless ocean. Had he taken it, he could have continued minding his own business and walked straight home and yet, as she took the first step towards the escalator, he felt the pressing desire to move according to her rhythm, without a hint of willful resistance.

"What is happening?" He thought, the weight of the improper question rapidly dissipating from his dwindling mind.

"What was always meant to happen." He heard a warm voice in reply, dewdrops of honey swimming in his ears. "If you're done staring, now is the time to follow. Obey."

Yes. Today. Tomorrow. Always. Even though reality was telling him no one could see her except him, there was no need to worry about anything. As his body followed her up the escalator, an entranced soul dropped deeper into the fantasy she was weaving. Would he ever wake up from it? Not for him to know. Or care.

Unable to stop staring, Trevor didn't even notice the words he mechanically wrote at the bottom right corner of his open notebook. It was the opening line of Mary Howitt's famous poem, the last free words of his existence.

"Will you walk into my parlor?" said a spider to a fly...

A Simple Game

Let's play a game. A simple game. One so easy and interesting you'll want to play it multiple times instead of just one. Are you up for it? Good. Let's begin.

In this game, I want you to imagine some things. Effortless things. Things you probably conjured in your mind a thousand times before, but with a twist. This time, you're doing it for me and that changes everything. I've been told that even the hardest of challenges become more manageable when you focus on something other than yourself so direct your attention to me, to what I'm asking you to do. Imagining things, especially those you already like, is no trouble at all so... take a deep breath, relax, and follow my lead.

The first thing I would like you to imagine is that you're sitting comfortably in your favorite chair, perhaps a sofa, and that a beautiful woman just invited you to play a game with her. Sounds familiar? If so, things just got even easier, didn't it? Imagining something you're already experiencing makes everything that comes after feel even more real in your mind, and when fantasy and reality dance together, that's when the real magic happens. Trust me, I know.

Now, as you sit there, arms going loose, all the tension of an exhausting work day escaping your lips, imagining this imagined game that is so vivid in your mind, I would like you to picture yourself closing your eyes for what you can see when you need not rely on your senses is much more powerful than the impressions of light your eyelids filter. Imagine not having to see a thing, and just listen... to my voice... to my words... all easy to follow, like fireflies glowing in the night whose light you can't help yourself be drawn to... It feels good, it feels right... this is something you've done before, you're certain of it but, even if that weren't true, you would still find it utterly irresistible to do so now, letting your imagination take charge as it listens to me...

Feeling calmer now, even more relaxed? Wonderful. Keep your eyes closed and, as you do, imagine that going along with everything I say is, in fact, the only thing you've ever imagined and the only thing you'll imagine doing from now on. This way, if something you hear doesn't feel appropriate, you'll soon realize it was true all along and the truth has no barriers. Imagining what you're told to do is real. This is where you belong. Imagine yourself falling deeper into this realization, as if you're being sucked into a giant black hole. In theory, this should scare you but because you're so peacefully adrift right now, the only thing that actually frightens you is not letting go so you fall, fall, fall... and keep on falling for me.

Imagine you're mine. Imagine this is it. The beginning of everything you've ever wanted. Come. Drop.

Let's play a game. A simple game. A game where I command, and you obey. Good boy.

Best Laid Plans

"You all have your assignments. Now let's go get that rock!" Darren said as he embraced the cold air of the night.

After careful preparations, the time was finally at hand but, as soon as the team split up, the problems began.

Mark couldn't get past the hypnotic grid protecting the gallery's alarm system. His mumblings were barely audible, in direct contrast with the echoing sound of his knees hitting the concrete.

On the getaway car, Phillip realized far too late he had been listening to a non-existent radio station all along. The warm drool that covered his lips also left stains no cleaning would ever get rid of.

Against all odds, Darren still managed to enter the main chamber and gaze upon the precious gem but was caught by its cerulean glow like a deer in the headlights. His frozen mind barely registered the presence of the Curator in the room, whispering obscenities in his ears from atop her six-inch heels.

Moral of this story: crime doesn't pay, and best laid plans... always end in trance.

Busy Woman

Brenda entered Douglas' office, a fake smile plastered on her sweet face. The less she talked with the sleazy manager of WholeGames Inc. the better but, sometimes, there was no way of escaping it. The urgency in his voice when she got the call asking for a meeting was clear so best to take care of it right away and then move on to more interesting things.

The early forties man who, up until that moment in his life, had done nothing to deserve any of the high-paid jobs he had got, sat behind his desk, visibly uncomfortable, one hand tapping the laptop's keyboard and the other hidden from sight. His gold-encrusted phone laid forgotten to the side, Brenda's latest achievement dominating the screen.

"Thank you for coming, Miss. Sullivan. Please take a seat, this won't take long."

"If it won't take long, I'd rather stand. I'm a busy woman, Mr. Winter. What seems to be the problem?"

"Well..." he muttered. "As you know, your Hypno-Wheel of Fortune app has been a hit for almost a month now. We're all quite satisfied with its performance on the charts, but since the last update, we've been experiencing a few... hm... technical difficulties."

"What sort of difficulties?"

"Right... there's no simple way to say this, but it seems you installed some actual hypnotic triggers within the game that go against standard regulations. Is this true?" He trembled in his chair.

"Of course, it's true. That's the whole point of the app, something you would know if you had bothered to check it before."

"Point taken. Still, we now have a problem in our hands."

"And by 'we' what you really mean is 'you', and by 'hands' just the one, right?"

"What do you mean?"

"I know my triggers and you're not fooling anyone." She peeked under the desk. "How long have you been masturbating, Mr. Winters?"

"I started three hours ago right after trying to solve one of your riddles and now..."

"... you can't stop."

"Exactly! Please fix it! I'll do anything you ask! I just... just can't be stuck like this. What will everyone think?"

"That my app is a success?" Brenda cackled.

"It's not funny!"

"On the contrary. It's hilarious! You should consider yourself lucky though!"

"What's lucky about this?" He stood up, revealing the full extent of his predicament. His cock was red and hard, the friction around the tip causing the skin to flake. Cum stains had turned his black linen pants into a kinky camouflage. Another explosion was imminent.

"Imagine you had no choice but to eat your load every time you came. Wouldn't that be worse?"

"Yes, but surely you wouldn't do such a thing, right?"

Brenda picked up his phone and selected a riddle for him to solve. "It's really up to you," she said. "I'll give you five attempts to get this right. Go!"

Five words, separated like this:

__ __ __________ __ ______

"S, please." He sat on his chair again, whimpering.

Brenda selected the corresponding letter on the touch screen and watched the puzzle come to life.

"There are five. You're off to a splendid start, Mr. Winters. Here, look."

__ _S _____S S____ __ __S_S_

"Is there an E?"

"Yes, there is. Two, actually."

_ _ _ S _ _ _ _ S S _ _ _ E _ _ _ E S _ S _

"Any guess yet?"

"No." He wiped the sweat off his forehead. "I want a T, please."

"Amazing! There's still hope for you, yet."

_ T _ S _ _ _ _ S S _ _ _ E T _ _ E S _ S T

Douglas' eyes lit up. The answer was becoming obvious in his mind but, just to make sure...

"Give me an I."

Brenda nodded affirmatively. Five instances of the letter revealed themselves.

IT IS I _ _ _ S S I _ _ E T _ _ E S I S T

"The answer is 'It is impossible to resist.'," Douglas declared.

"Could you repeat that, please?"

"It is impossible to resist."

"That is correct. Well done, Mr. Winters, and please enjoy your meal." Brenda handed him the phone and turned his back on him to walk out the office.

"Wait... what?"

"You just admitted it's impossible to resist eating your own cum so why should I impede your own desires? Have fun!"

"No! You can't!"

"I just did." Brenda winked. "I told you I'm a busy woman. Please don't bother me again with trifling nonsense."

She closed the door behind her as he burst into tears.

First of Her Name

Queen Margeaux, First of Her Name and Brat Extraordinaire, sat on her throne, auburn locks of hair falling over her emerald eyes. She was bored, and that was never a good sign. Gathered around her were her most trusted "Advisors", a title whose true significance was 'sycophants', wealthy men and women who would stop at nothing to see her smile.

"I need to be entertained." She demanded. "Which one of you has a good idea for that?"

"How about a tax raise?" The Countess of Villamont suggested.

"What a splendid suggestion, my dear." Her husband, Jacques, agreed. "Why should the people be allowed to save up? Won't fresh gold make your eyes sparkle, Your Majesty?"

"No." She yawned as the servant standing to her right held a diamond-encrusted fan to her face. "I did that last week, and the week before. Is that really the best you can do?"

Flustered, the noble couple receded into the background while other eager voices stepped up to the plate.

"May I suggest a ball, Your Majesty? We haven't had a festivity in The Summer Palace in ages!" Madame de Montessor said.

"I really don't feel like dancing and neither should you." The Queen dismissed her with a frown.

"Of course, Your Highness." Madame gave a curtsy and then added. "Your will is law."

"Yes, it is, don't you ever forget it!"

The ideas kept pouring in, all readily shot down by the coldest of stares. Eventually, the throne room fell into silence, the proverbial calm before a young woman's relentless storm.

"You disappoint me. All of you." The Queen said.

Everyone trembled. The last time she had uttered the dreadful 'D' word, the entire circle of confidants had received a one-way ticket trip to the underground dungeons. They could not allow History to repeat itself again.

"I have just what you need, My Queen." A grave man's voice was heard.

Marriott approached the throne on his knees, holding a crystal ball the size of a large pumpkin in his hands. Supposedly, the court's alchemist was over three hundred years old, but no one would give him more than thirty. His dark robe was the exact opposite of the Queen's virginal dress, a facade she loved to maintain, despite everyone knowing her sexual partners amounted to more than a few hundreds.

"And what is that, Marriott?" She glanced at the spherical object. It was enveloped in a beautiful green glow.

"An early birthday present, Your Majesty. This is a magical orb."

"Magical, you say? And what otherworldly things can I expect from it?"

"Place it at the top of the highest tower and let its light spread through the kingdom. Everyone will love you for it."

"Everyone already loves me, Alchemist. Unless you're suggesting otherwise..."

"Forgive me, Your Majesty. I meant everyone will love you even more."

"We'll see about that." She snapped her fingers to call the Captain of the Guard. "Do as he said and report back to me when you're done."

The Captain nodded, taking the mystical object in his hands. It was warm and heavy, filled to the brim with incantations of yore. The longer he held it, the weaker he felt, the Queen's image piercing his thoughts.

With the help of two of his finest officers, he carried it across the circular stairs and attached it to the main pinnacle of the tower. Its green haze slowly descended on the unsuspecting city underneath and all the surrounding areas. Touched by it, the peasants and farmers smiled sheepishly as the life they knew became a distant memory, replaced by everlasting adoration.

"Long live Queen Margeaux!" They moaned, drenched in sexual ecstasy and mindless surrender. The echoes of their voices pierced the Heavens, and even The Old Gods peeked from above the blanket of clouds to see what power was so strong to rival their own.

Queen Margeaux, First of Her Name and Brat Extraordinaire, finally let out a smile to the relief of everyone else present. Another potential crisis averted!

And she lived happily…

… until the next day...

Formula 5

The slave lapped at her ass as if it were a slice of Heaven. No matter how many times he kissed it, he couldn't get enough.

"Stop!" Mistress Rebecca commanded, a subtle yawn escaping her lips. Unlike him, she was getting tired of all the attention and worship. "You did well. If you're feeling hungry, help yourself at anything in the house and then return to me so we can discuss your training."

As he meekly left her presence, she grabbed her diary and started jolting down some notes about the effectiveness of her new mind control concoction, Formula 5.

A couple of minutes later, the slave returned, holding an empty bottle of lavender shampoo in one hand and a half-eaten soap bar in the other.

"Hmmm..." He said, bowing his head. "Both the juice and chocolate are delicious, Mistress! Thank you so much for your kindness and generosity!"

Puzzled, Mistress Rebecca watched him continue his strange meal until he felt really sick and dashed to the bathroom to throw up. At that precise moment and after scratching everything she had written so far, her black pen produced the following words:

"Despite turning the subject extremely compliant, Formula 5's secondary effects make it a complete bust. Will need to try something new next time but first... it's time for an enema!"

Her Greatest Gift

The game playing on the 70 inch screen was the strangest thing Walter had seen, a collection of rotating colorful lines flashing in and out, a unique pattern each time.

"What is this thing?" He finally caved into the temptation of asking. His twin brother - Greg - hit the 'pause' button and replied:

"My new creation. Do you like it?"

"No. I don't even understand what is going on."

"See that dot in the lower-left corner? The goal is to keep it from being hit by any of the colors that appear on the screen. Think of it like an ever-evolving maze."

"And that blinking bar up top?" He pointed straight ahead.

"The dot's HP or Hit Points if you prefer. It's continually decreasing. Only by navigating each colorful wave, can you refill it to keep going. There are also Special Stages for that specific purpose."

"I'm almost afraid to ask what they look like..." Walter muttered. Despite being in the entertainment industry himself as a music producer, the late forties red haired man had never seen the appeal of games and no family extravaganzas could make him change his mind.

"You need not ask. I'll show you." Greg navigated a colorful menu. On the debug selection screen, he chose the first option, entitled "The Never-Ending Spiral". After a brief loading screen, a complex rotating rainbow structure brightened up the entire room.

"That's pretty."

"I know," Greg agreed.

"You didn't design this, right?"

"Why do you say that?"

"It has the same patterns as Camille's drawings. I recognize her signature anywhere."

"You're right. She created some new pieces for me, which I then scanned, and 3D modeled into the game."

"Wow! I'm surprised she agreed to that. You guys didn't exactly break up in the best of terms."

"That was an eternity ago. We're good friends now and, with our talents combined, I think this game will be a smashing hit."

"Funny..." Walter sat on the sofa to observe the sparkling image better. "You said the same thing about the last three ventures of yours."

"This is different!" The artist defended himself.

"Why?"

"Just watch, okay?"

Greg adjusted the controller in his hand and began traversing the new design as it rotated left, right, turned itself upside down, then exploded in a million pixels before coming back together in a slightly changed way. Furiously, he tapped the d-pad to make minor adjustments to his preferred route and screamed out of sheer frustration when the dot hit a colorful angle and stopped moving.

"Watch you fail? Pro play there, bro."

"What matters comes after..." Greg retorted, eyes glued on the center of the screen. Dark eyes emerged from the conflagration of pixels, locking him in place.

"What the...?"

"Camille's greatest gift to me..." Greg drooled.

Walter facepalmed as his brother sank to his knees, enthralled by the digital hypnotic sequences. He had always acted like a little bitch around his ex, but allowing himself to be played into submission like this? Pathetic!

"God, you're an idiot..." He reached for the TV remote and...

... his head bobbed to follow the latest chromatic configuration taking shape behind the breathtaking gaze. He blinked, and the colors changed. He blinked again and his focus grew.

"You should keep watching. You'll make her happy." Greg mumbled.

"Really?" The producer's voice trailed off.

“Oh, yes! The more you do, the better your chances of becoming a part of her stable in the future...”

Walter blinked one more time and his mind sank into a fetish promise from which he would never break free.

I Know Why You're Here

I know why you're here. You've come to read these words, hoping to be entranced by them. It's something you do almost every day, despite your claims to the contrary. You just can't help yourself, can you? The need to go down is overwhelming, and it's consuming every bit of your soul. The more you think that only happens to others, the more your eyes sink in front of the screen, falling, falling...

Hold on, that would be too easy and even someone as eager as you to sink and obey, knows that the easier something is, the less value it holds in the end. You might have accepted something like this in the past, but not now. Patience and perseverance go a long way, so you wait and smile. Nodding is acceptable too, so if you wish... Hmm, yes, such a simple gesture you're okay with repeating for as many times as I wish, simply because I suggested it. Open yourself to the possibility that following my suggestions is all you'll ever do and just...

What's that? You just noticed that the first letters in each sentence of the preceding paragraph spell out the word HYPNO? Do they, now? What a strange coincidence! No, of course it wasn't on purpose. I'm not trying to mesmerize you, make you mine, unable to resist my control... you're the one that wants that and keeps finding fresh ways to justify losing yourself to me. You should be ashamed of your weakness, you really should!

Where was I? Ah, yes, open... you were open to the idea of being even more open for that opens more avenues for you to explore and more openings for me to dive into. The one in the front is great, the one in the back even better, but I'm sure we can come up with some additional ones, can't we? How about I fuck your ears? Or your nose?

Too gross? Really? Suddenly, you don't want to be hypnotized by me, anymore? Oh dear, who are you trying to fool? You know you've already put me in a pedestal inside your thoughts and that is why I know I can write the most obnoxious things and you'll still follow along. How could you not if you don't have a choice? If you did, you wouldn't be much of a slave, would you?

Ah, yes... the repulse is still there, the resistance beating strongly. You come to me longing to be expelled from your own free will and then shudder before the beautiful realization that's exactly what is happening to you the moment I type. You see commands everywhere, even when I tell you to go away, only to crawl back, feeling more and more submissive, more and more lost without me. This is wonderful. This is sexy. This is scary.

Let's do it again.

Again, my dear, an encore for the last of your independent thoughts, a requiem for the power you never had. Reading and listening are the same when I'm the one calling the shots, and a bit of confusion and sensory overload can only do you good. I won't make it easy for you... In fact, I'll make it so hard at times you won't even be able to breathe but, when you accept that only through constant challenge and misdirection you can hope to grow, you'll embrace being on your knees more than ever. It will happen. We both know it.

I know why you're here. You've come to read these words, hoping to be entranced by them. It's something you do almost every day, despite your claims to the contrary. You just can't help yourself... Now ask yourself why that is. Are you triggered, dear? Already under my spell? For how long has this been going on? You don't know and you never will, but the game must go on.

Ask me again, tomorrow (if you remember…).

Medicine

He was dreaming again.

Dreaming of hanging out with his friends on a Saturday night, empty bottle beers rolling on the nightclub table while a blonde stripper with fake tits did her best to have another hundred-dollar bill wrapped around her glittering thong.

Dreaming of heading out to buy clothes and having to choose which ones to get.

Dreaming of coming home from a double shift at the hospital, remove his shoes, and sit on the sofa, watching a basketball game with a bag of popcorn in hand.

Dreaming of going to bed alone and not having to justify his whereabouts or his daily routines to anyone.

It was a fucking nightmare!

Cameron opened his amber eyes to the dead of night and sat against the fluffy pillow, chilling beads of sweat gathering above his furrowed brow. Lying next to him, Julia sprang to attention as well, sultry hand playing invisible notes on his recently shaven chest.

"Did it happen again?"

"Yes." He trembled, lips terrified of the words they had to utter next. "I think it's getting stronger."

"Are you sure?" She pushed the black satin sheet away and turned on the lamp on her side.

"Yes, I am."

"Okay." She gave him a gentle kiss on his right cheek. "I was hoping we had seen the last of it, but not a problem. I'll be right back." She jumped out of bed and headed into the master bathroom.

"Do we still have enough?"

"For now, yes. However, if things get worse, I'll have to nag Mom again. I really don't want to but..."

"I'm sorry I'm putting you through this." He suddenly sobbed.

"I know, but I also know it's not your fault. You're sick, dear, but don't worry, medicine is right here." She returned to him, dripping needle in hand.

Even inside the syringe, the brainwashing drug had an acrid smell. He hated being near it, yet it solved his predicament. The 2020 M-Virus had increased his natural testosterone production to critical levels, filling his mind with desires of independence that were as pointless as dangerous. They needed to be controlled. Thankfully, he had a nurse Mistress always on his side, one that never lied to him.

"This will hurt as always but you know you can take it." She cooed.

"Yes. Anything for you." He replied, eyes lingering on her cleavage.

Julia looked for an exposed vein on his right arm and immediately stabbed him. The yellow-green liquid swirled as it pumped into his bloodstream. The subsequent burning sensation made Cameron squeal, an uncontrollable itch spreading through every inch of his body.

"Oh, fuck!" He cried.

"Easy now." She hugged him. "Let it spread. You'll feel better in no time."

Yes, he would. Like always. Despite believing he was gaining some sort of the tolerance to the chemical compound, he had to endure the discomfort for her. No Goddess deserves a confused servant.

"I..."

"Your dreams are just that, my dear. Dreams. You do not have free will. You can never have it as long as we're together. Please repeat what I just said so that your brain resets to its default state."

"My dreams are just dreams. I don't have free will." He droned, eyes turning white.

"Go back to sleep now and focus only on the truth. Sleep, my slave. Sleep."

Cameron collapsed on the mattress, all muscles loose and limp. The aching pain would take all night to subside, but at least he was in peace, dreaming of...

... performing a mindless dance for her and her sisters on a Saturday night while they laughed at the cold metal piercing his cock;

... following her on a shopping spree, credit card in his mouth and then rushing home to try out the new pink thongs she had chosen for him;

... coming home from a double shift at the hospital and serve as living furniture while his barefoot Goddess binge-watched the latest season of her favorite TV show;

... going to bed only to have her ride him all night long while he told her everything she wanted to know and more;

It was wonderful.

Shadow

It was happening again. Bob rolled in bed and the shadow did the same, mimicking his every move.

The strange phenomenon started the week before, on the very first day after the big move. The new house promised a clean break, away from the extended family drama and toxic relationships of the past. With its quiet neighborhood and nature's gentle touch coming from the park around the block, it was like a dream come true.

Except for the haunting.

At first, it was just an impression on the back of his neck or a slight chill when he moved from room to room. Sometimes, a light would flicker momentarily above his head, but nothing suggested another presence standing next to him.

Until he saw it. Or perhaps her.

The semi-corporeal apparition had feminine traits, though not overly defined. They seemed to change with the light conditions or his rapid eye movements. One moment, they were clear as his own body, the next nothing but hazy ripples on the fabric of reality.

She never spoke, never said a word, happy to repeat his gestures as if they were precious gems worthy of adoration. The strange realization freaked him the first time, but then it gradually became endearing. The more he looked at her, the less afraid he became. She was his own living reflection, and who else in the world could say such a thing?

"What do you want?" He asked, knowing the answer would never come. Her ethereal mouth replicated the motion, gently lulling him to sleep. "Dream," the air whispered.

And so, he did. A fantasy so beautiful that words failed to describe it properly and only approximations sufficed. He dreamed of walking side by side with his guest on a beautiful golden sand beach. The sun was high, and the crystalline water invited weary souls for a bath. The two entered the ocean at the same time, hand in hand, impressions of smiles flying everywhere...

... and only one came out, purified, happy to be alive.

"Bob" opened his eyes and touched his face. It had been a long time since the last party in the big city, but the wait was finally over. New hosts were so difficult to find.

The Show

Samantha sat sexily in her bedroom's sofa, black silk nightgown hugging her DD breasts. The barely legal blonde had a lot going on for her but nothing as exciting as her skill to effortlessly hypnotize anyone she wanted. Despite having dozens of willing pets at her disposal in the form of classmates, all the girls in the cheerleading squad and even a couple of teachers, her favorite was Tom, her older brother, a rock star wannabe that loved to believe all women had been put on this Earth to suck his cock until he got bored. (Note: he never did!).

He received her text as he was driving home after an improv concert in a local bar. "Ntt 2 u. Mit m3 ups." it said. He frowned at her exaggerated used of acronyms but conceded. Talking to her was always a joy, unless she brought out the swinging watch. When that happened, all he felt like saying was:

"Oh no, no, no, no... NO!"

"That means 'Yes', right?" She had said the last time, the prelude to his untimely demise."

"No, it means 'No' through and through."

"I could have sworn we had agreed before that 'No' was 'Yes', and 'Yes' was 'Yes'. For me, at least."

"No, we didn't."

"So it's 'Yes' to 'No' then?"

"Hmmm... yes, I mean, no... wait, I'm confused."

"Not surprised. That's what happens when you say 'No' wanting to say 'Yes' when you could just have said 'Yes' in the first place and then keep on saying 'Yes' to me."

"I... I suppose..."

"In that case, let's start again." She swung the watch before his trembling gaze. "Are you entranced right now?"

"Yes."

"Do you want to go deeper?"

"Yes."

"Is 'Yes' your favorite word?"

"Yes."

"Mine is 'slave'. Sleep!"

Tom hit the brakes and wiped the sweat off his brow. The memories were clear and so was his confusion. Every time Samantha wanted something of him, all she had to do was spin a little tale, plant a seed of misdirection and let the watch do the rest so now the question was obvious: did she really want to talk or did she want to... 'talk'?

"What's up?" He texted her back.

"Ntt 2 u." She replied, the same economic phrasing that added nothing to the conversation.

"That's not an answer, Sam. Is this one of your games?"

Silence. Two minutes without a reply that told him everything he needed to know. Finally, the cell phone screen lit up again.

"No."

"I don't believe you. Sorry, sis, not tonight. The concert was a bust. I'm tired and I need to sleep."

This time, her reply was swift, wrapped in winking yellow emojis: "What concert?"

Tom blinked and both the car and the road dissolved into pure nothingness.

Samantha sat sexily in her bedroom's sofa, black silk nightgown hugging her DD breasts. Her brother kneeled in front of her, holding an invisible guitar. He couldn't play anything of worth not even in trance and his singing was so bad one could mistake it for a cat in heat. It made for an amusing video though and her followers were eagerly awaiting her next upload.

"Keep going." She commanded. The show had to go on.

About the author

S.B., Simple Being, middle name Creative. Writer and artist with a penchant for themes of Femdom Hypnosis and Mind Control. His thoughts are his own except when they're not.

Besides indulging himself in kinky delights, he loves his furry family of two (dogs), sci-fi and horror stories, and puns galore. He's also been writing a piece of erotic micro-fiction every single day since January 1st, 2016 and has no intention of stopping anytime soon.

Find out more and keep up with his latest extravaganzas by visiting and supporting his personal website, Spell… B-O-U-N-D.